This Little Tiger book belongs to:

CAT

~~Dog~~

000001045387

LITTLE TIGER PRESS
1 The Coda Centre, 189 Munster Road, London SW6 6AW
www.littletiger.co.uk

First published in Great Britain 2016
This edition published 2016

Concept by Dana Brown and Maudie Powell-Tuck
Text by Maudie Powell-Tuck
Text copyright © Little Tiger Press 2016
Illustrations copyright © Richard Smythe 2016
Richard Smythe has asserted his right to be identified as the illustrator
of this work under the Copyright, Designs and Patents Act, 1988

A CIP catalogue record for this book is available from the British Library

Printed in China · LTP/1800/1436/0216

2 4 6 8 10 9 7 5 3 1

For Dana, the other half of Team Messy Book
– M P T

For Henry, Darcey and Gertruda
– R S

The MESSY BOOK

Maudie Powell-Tuck • **Richard Smythe**

LITTLE TIGER PRESS
London

I've made a mess.

Maybe you should tidy it up?

Maybe. Or we **could just** . . .

Drat. The mess is back.
I can help you tidy, Cat. We can sing a tidy up song.
No. Let's JUMP on it.

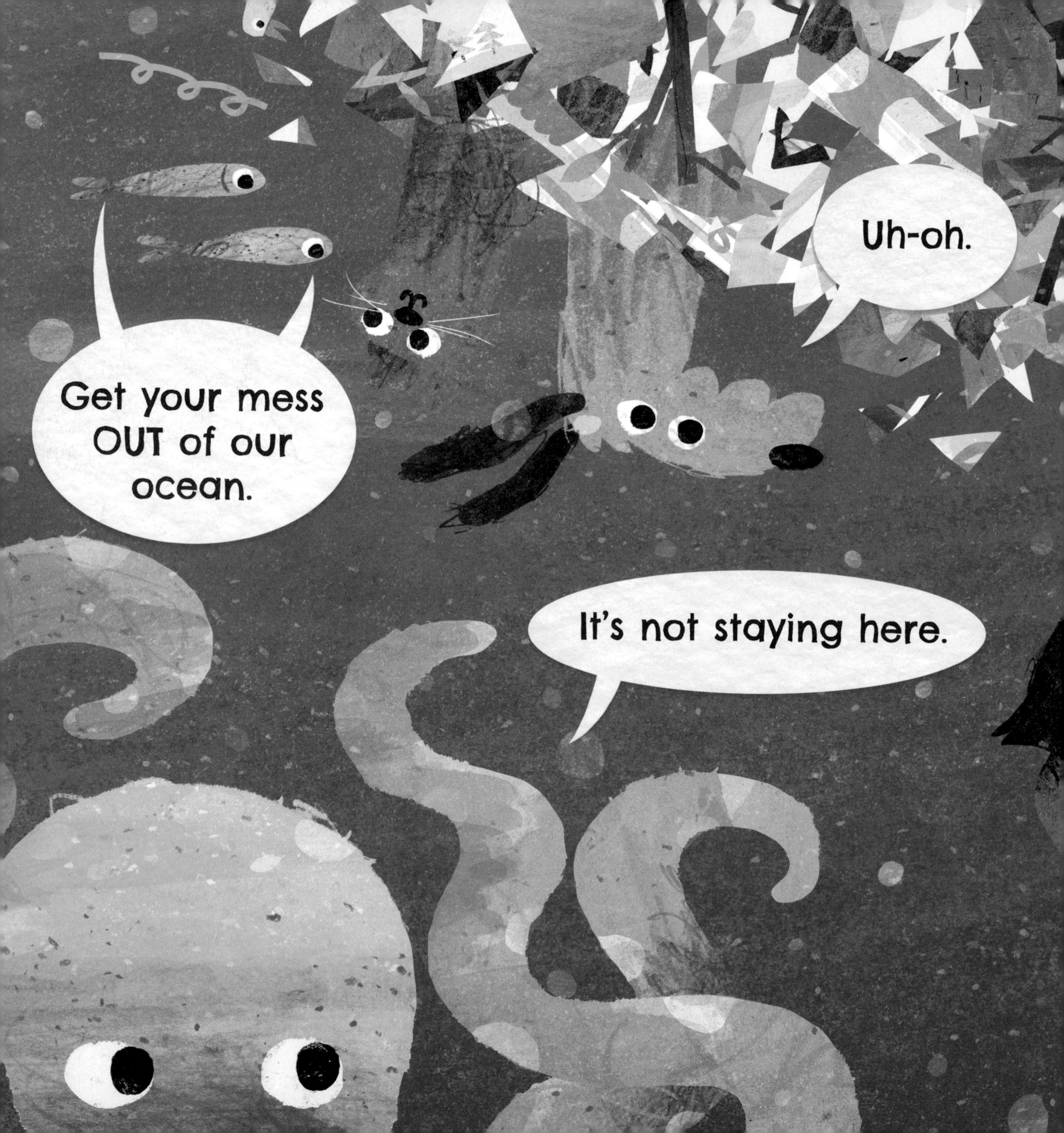
Get your mess OUT of our ocean.
Uh-oh.
It's not staying here.

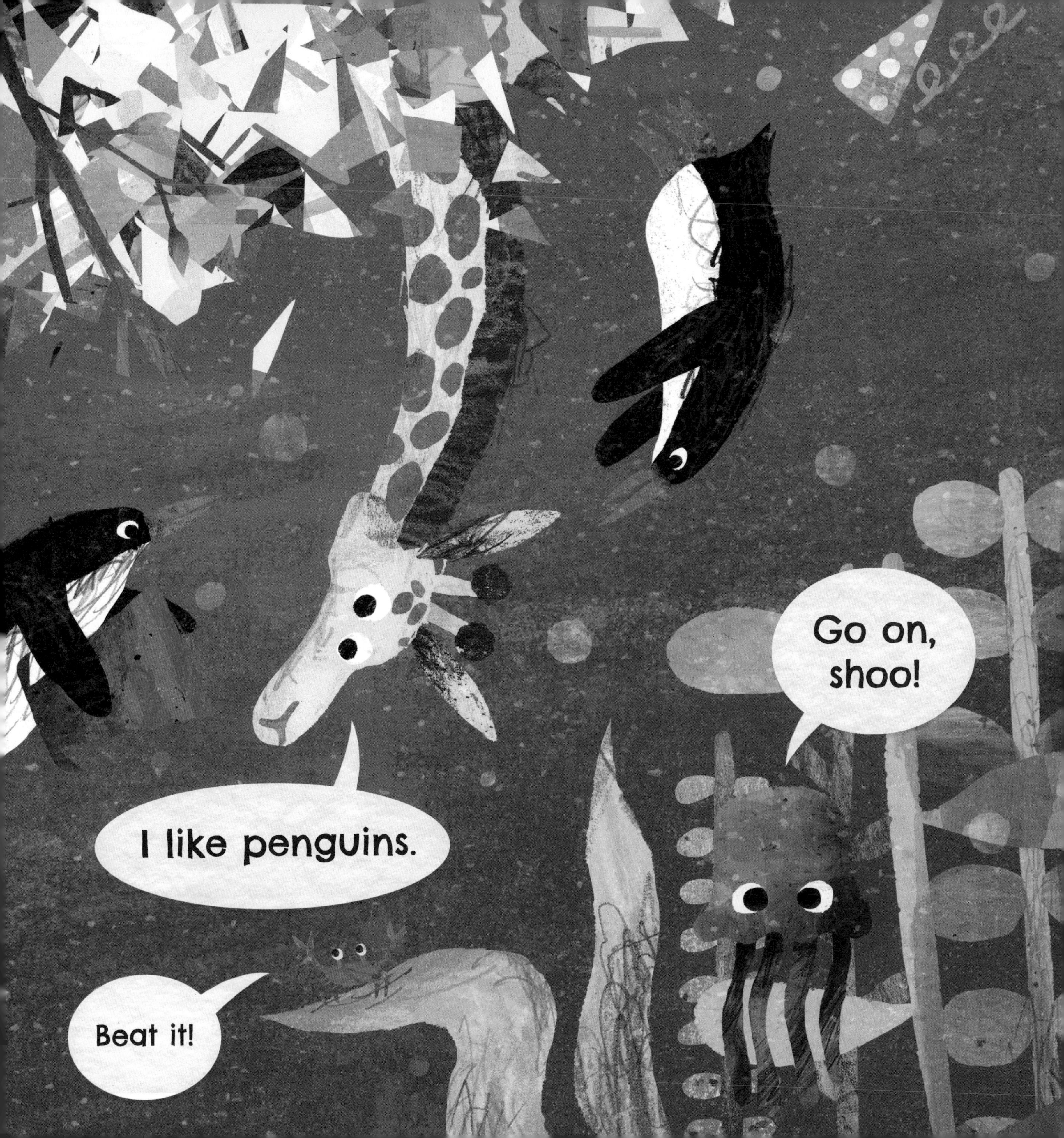

Go on, shoo!
I like penguins.
Beat it!

Ew. I'm wet.
And now the mess is soggy. Please, please, PLEASE can we tidy up?

But tidying is *boring.*

We could hide the mess under my bed . . .

or blow it up . . .

. . . or eat it.

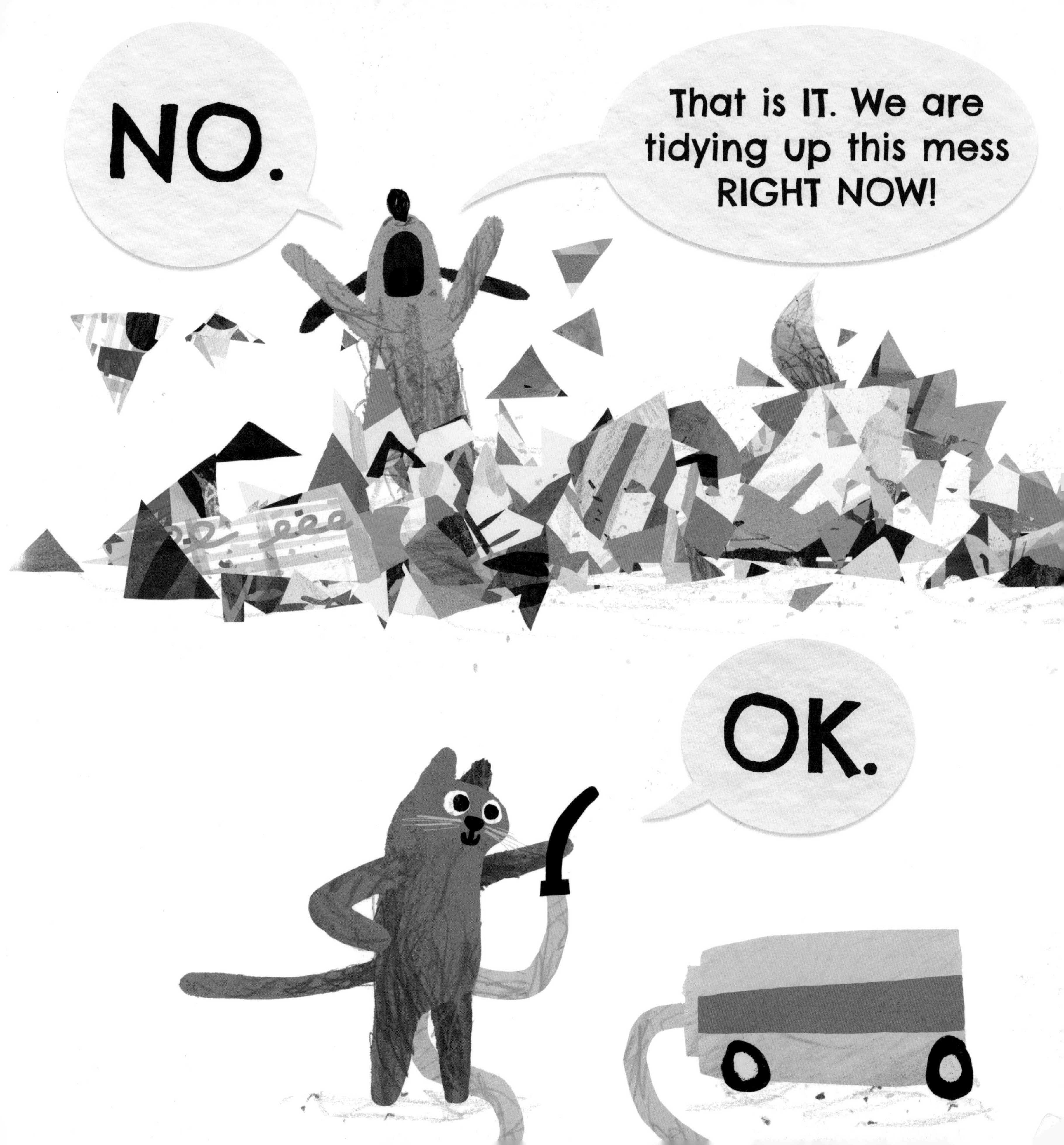
NO.
That is IT. We are tidying up this mess RIGHT NOW!
OK.

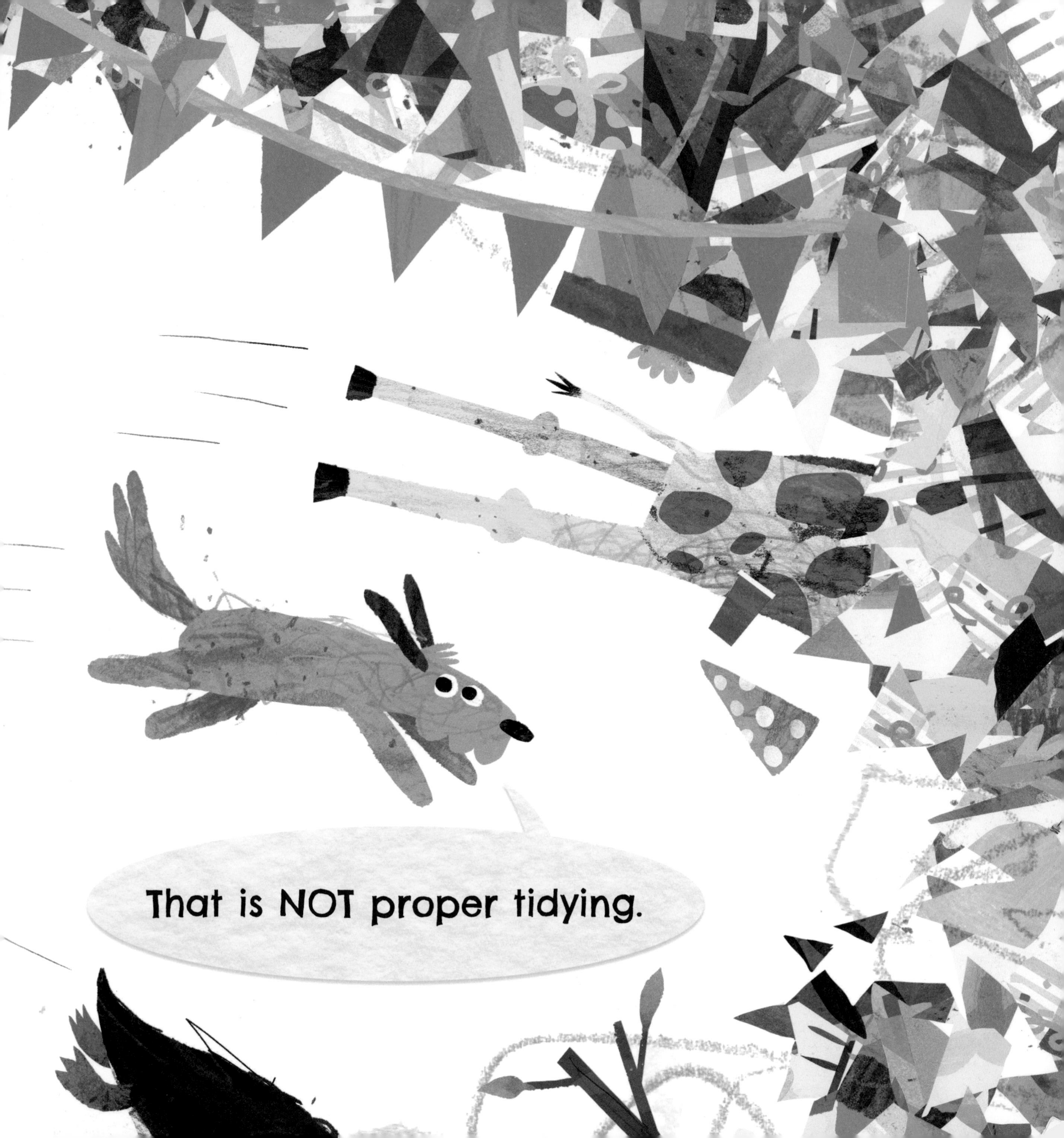
That is NOT proper tidying.

RUMBLE
RUMBLE
RUMBLE

That was FUN.
GRRRRRRRRRRRRRRRRRRRRRR!
I'm sorry, buddy. Let's tidy up.

Woo hoo! Everything is back where it belongs. No more mess!

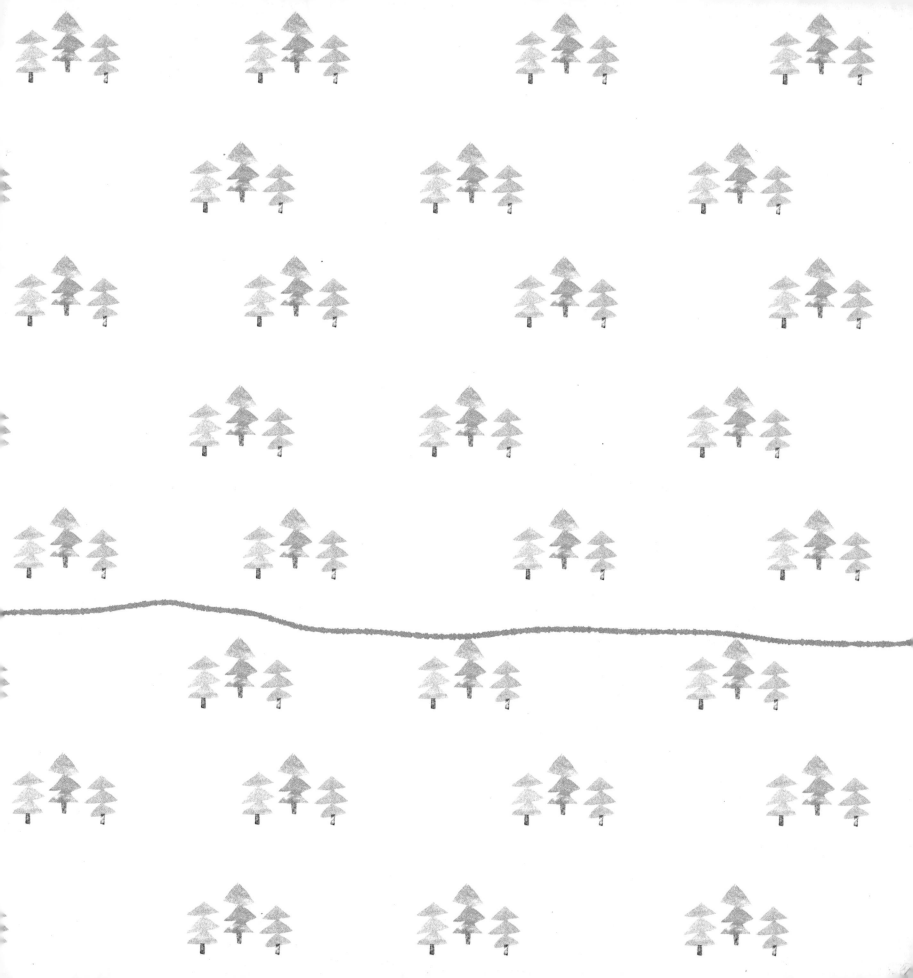

More tip-top reads from Little Tiger Press!

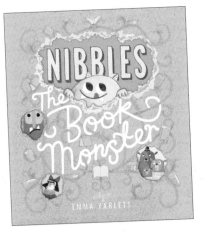

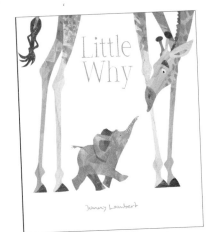

For information regarding any of the above titles
or for our catalogue, please contact us:
Little Tiger Press, 1 The Coda Centre,
189 Munster Road, London SW6 6AW
Tel: 020 7385 6333 · E-mail: contact@littletiger.co.uk
www.littletiger.co.uk